MOTHER GOOSE

MOTHER GOOSE
or the
OLD NURSERY RHYMES

Illustrated by
KATE GREENAWAY

About This Book

This new book has been specially created from three books illustrated by Kate Greenaway. The nursery rhymes up to "Ring-a-ring a-roses" on page 55 are the complete, unabridged content of *Mother Goose or the Old Nursery Rhymes* which was published in London in 1881 by George Routledge. Three extra illustrations for "Jack and Jill", "Mary, Mary" and "Little Miss Muffet" come from *The April Baby's Book of Tunes*. Pages 56 to 73 (from "Indeed it is True" to "My house is red") are from *Under the Window*, both written and illustrated by Kate Greenaway and first published in 1878 in London by George Routledge. "Little Polly Flinders" and the rhymes on the following pages are from *The April Baby's Book of Tunes*, written by Countess Russell, Mary von Arnim, and illustrated by Kate Greenaway. It was published in 1900 by Macmillan.

Kate Greenaway was born in 1846 and died in 1901.

The artwork has been restored to its original condition.

CONTENTS

KG

KG

Hark ! bark ! the dogs bark,
The beggars are coming to town;
Some in rags and some in tags,
And some in silken gowns.
Some gave them white bread,
And some gave them brown,
And some gave them a good horse-whip,
And sent them out of the town.

KG.

Little Jack Horner, sat in the corner,
Eating a Christmas pie;
He put in his thumb, and pulled out a plum,
And said, oh ! what a good boy am I.

There was an old woman
Lived under a hill;
And if she's not gone,
She lives there still.

Diddlty, diddlty, dumpty,
The cat run up the plum tree;
Give her a plum, and down she'll come,
Diddlty, diddlty, dumpty.

We're all jolly boys, and we're coming
    with a noise,
Our stockings shall be made
Of the finest silk,
And our tails shall touch the ground.

K.G.

To market, to market, to buy a plum cake,
Home again, home again, market is late;
To market, to market, to buy a plum bun,
Home again, home again, market is done.

Elsie Marley has grown so fine,
She won't get up to serve the swine;
But lies in bed till eight or nine,
And surely she does take her time.

Daffy-down-dilly has come up to town,
In a yellow petticoat and a green gown.

Jack Sprat could eat no fat,
His wife could eat no lean;
And so between them both,
They licked the platter clean.

Lucy Locket, lost her pocket,
Kitty Fisher found it;
There was not a penny in it,
But a ribbon round it.

KG

Cross Patch, lift the latch,
Sit by the fire and spin;
Take a cup, and drink it up,
Then call your neighbours in.

K. D

Johnny shall have a new bonnet,
And Johnny shall go to the fair;
And Johnny shall have a blue ribbon,
To tie up his bonny brown hair.

K.G

There was a little boy and a little girl
Lived in an alley;
Says the little boy to the little girl,
"Shall I, oh! shall I?"
Says the little girl to the little boy,
"What shall we do?"
Says the little boy to the little girl,
"I will kiss you!"

K.G.

Jack and Jill
Went up the hill,
To fetch a pail of water;

Jack fell down
And broke his crown,
And Jill came tumbling after.

Little Bo-peep has lost her sheep,
And can't tell where to find them;
Leave them alone, and they'll come home,
And bring their tails behind them.

Polly put the kettle on,
Polly put the kettle on,
Polly put the kettle on,
We'll all have tea.
Sukey take it off again,
Sukey take it off again,
Sukey take it off again,
They're all gone away.

Little Tommy Tittlemouse,
Lived in a little house;
He caught fishes
In other men's ditches.

Tell Tale Tit,
Your tongue shall be slit;
And all the dogs in the town
Shall have a little bit.

Goosey, goosey, gander,
Where shall I wander?
Up stairs, down stairs,
And in my lady's chamber:
There I met an old man,
Would not say his prayers;
Take him by the left leg,
Throw him down the stairs.

KG

Willy boy, Willy boy, where are you going?
I will go with you, if I may.
I'm going to the meadow to see them a
        mowing,
I'm going to help them make the hay.

Mary, Mary, quite contrary,
How does your garden grow?

With silver bells, and cockle shells,
And cowslips all of a row.

A diller, a dollar,
A ten o'clock scholar;
What makes you come so soon?
You used to come at ten o'clock,
But now you come at noon!

Little Betty Blue,
Lost her holiday shoe.
What will poor Betty do?
Why, give her another,
To match the other,
And then she will walk in two.

Billy boy blue, come blow me your horn,
The sheeps' in the meadow, the cows'
        in the corn;
Is that the way you mind your sheep,
Under the Haycock fast asleep?

Girls and boys come out to play,
The moon it shines, as bright as day;
Leave your supper, and leave your sleep,
And come to your playmates in the street;
Come with a whoop, come with a call,
Come with a good will, or come not at all;
Up the ladder and down the wall,
A halfpenny loaf will serve us all.

Here am I, little jumping Joan,
When nobody's with me,
I'm always alone.

Ride a cock-horse,
To Banbury-cross,
To see little Johnny
Get on a white horse.

K.G

37

Rock-a-bye baby,
Thy cradle is green;
Father's a nobleman,
Mother's a queen.
And Betty's a lady,
And wears a gold ring;
And Johnny's a drummer,
And drums for the king.

Little Tom Tucker,
He sang for his supper.
What did he sing for?
Why, white bread and butter.
How can I cut it without a knife?
How can I marry without a wife?

Little Miss Muffet,
Sat on a tuffet,
Eating some curds and whey;
There came a great spider,
And sat down beside her,
And frightened Miss Muffet away.

K.G

See-Saw-Jack in the hedge,
Which is the way to London-bridge?

Little lad, little lad,
Where wast thou born?
Far off in Lancashire,
Under a thorn;
Where they sup sour milk
From a ram's horn.

As I was going up Pippin Hill,
Pippin Hill was dirty;
There I met a sweet pretty lass,
And she dropped me a curtsey.

Little maid, little maid,
Whither goest thou?
Down in the meadow
To milk my cow.

My mother, and your mother,
Went over the way;
Said my mother, to your mother,
"It's chop-a-nose day."

All around the green gravel,
The grass grows so green,
And all the pretty maids are fit to be seen;
Wash them in milk,
Dress them in silk,
And the first to go down shall be married.

K.G

One foot up, the other foot down,
That's the way to London-town.

K.G

Georgie Peorgie, pudding and pie,
Kissed the girls and made them cry;
When the girls begin to play,
Georgie Peorgie runs away.

KG.

As Tommy Snooks, and Bessie Brooks
Were walking out one Sunday;
Says Tommy Snooks to Bessie Brooks,
"To-morrow — will be Monday."

K.G.

Tom, Tom, the piper's son,
He learnt to play when he was young,
He with his pipe made such a noise,
That he pleased all the girls and boys.

K.G

Ring-a-ring-a-roses,
A pocket full of posies;
Hush! hush! hush! hush!
We're all tumbled down.

Draw a pail of water,
For my lady's daughter;
My father's a king, and my mother's a queen,
My two little sisters are dressed in green,
Stamping grass and parsley,
Marigold leaves and daisies.
One rush! two rush!
Pray thee, fine lady, come under my bush.

KG

Bonny lass, pretty lass, wilt thou be mine?
Thou shalt not wash dishes,
Nor yet serve the swine;
Thou shalt sit on a cushion, and sew a
        fine seam,
And thou shalt eat strawberries, sugar,
        and cream!

Humpty Dumpty sat on a wall,
Humpty Dumpty had a great fall.

Indeed it is true, it is perfectly true;
    Believe me, indeed, I am playing no tricks;
An old man and his dog bide up there in the moon,
    And he's cross as a bundle of sticks.

K.G

School is over,
Oh, what fun!
Lessons finished, —
Play begun.
Who'll run fastest,
You or I?
Who'll laugh loudest? —
Let us try.

K.G.

Five little sisters walking in a row;
Now, isn't that the best way for little girls to go?
Each had a round hat, each had a muff,
And each had a new pelisse of soft green stuff.

Five little marigolds standing in a row;
Now, isn't that the best way for marigolds to grow?
Each with a green stalk, and all the five had got
A bright yellow flower, and a new red pot.

You are going out to tea to-day,
    So mind how you behave;
Let all accounts I have of you
    Be pleasant ones, I crave.

Don't spill your tea, or gnaw your bread,
    And don't tease one another;
And Tommy mustn't talk too much,
    Or quarrel with his brother.

Say "If you please," and "Thank you, Nurse;"
    Come home at eight o'clock;
And, Fanny, pray be careful that
    You do not tear your frock.

Now mind your manners, children five,
    Attend to what I say;
And then, perhaps, I'll let you go
    Again another day.

Up you go, shuttlecocks, ever so high!
Why come you down again, shuttlecocks—why?
When you have got so far, why do you fall?—
Where all are high, which is highest of all?

Higgledy, piggledy! see how they run!
Hopperty, popperty! what is the fun?
Has the sun or the moon tumbled into the sea?
What is the matter, now? Pray tell it me!

Higgledy, piggledy! how can I tell?
Hopperty, popperty! hark to the bell!
The rats and the mice even scamper away;
Who can say what may not happen to-day?

K.C

Which is the way to Somewhere Town?
   Oh, up in the morning early;
Over the tiles and the chimney-pots,
   That is the way, quite clearly.

And which is the door to Somewhere Town?
   Oh, up in the morning early;
The round red sun is the door to go through,
   That is the way, quite clearly.

Pipe thee high, and pipe thee low,
Let the little feet go faster;
Blow your penny trumpet, — blow!
Well done, little master!

Bowl away! bowl away!
   Fast as you can;
He who can fastest bowl,
   He is my man!

Up and down, round about, —
   Don't let it fall;
Ten times, or twenty times,
   Beat, beat them all!

KG

I saw a ship that sailed the sea,
    It left me as the sun went down;
The white birds flew, and followed it
    To town, — to London town.

Right sad where we to stand alone,
    And see it pass so far away;
And yet we knew some ship would come —
    Some other ship — some other day.

It was Tommy who said,
    "The sweet spring-time is come;
I see the birds flit,
    And I hear the bees hum.

"Oho! Mister Lark,
    Up aloft in the sky,
Now, which is the happiest, —
    Is it you, sir, or I?"

"Shall I sing?" says the Lark,
   "Shall I bloom?" says the Flower;
"Shall I come?" says the Sun,
   "Or shall I?" says the Shower.

Sing your song, pretty Bird,
   Roses, bloom for an hour;
Shine on, dearest Sun,
   Go away, naughty Shower!

Little Miss Patty and Master Paul
Have found two snails on the garden wall.
"These snails," said Paul, "how slow they walk! —
A great deal slower than we can talk.
Make haste, Mr. Snail, travel quicker, I pray;
In a race with our tongues you'd be beaten to-day."

Now, all of you, give heed unto
   The tale I now relate,
About two girls and one small boy,
   A cat, and a green gate.

*   *   *   *   *   *

Alack! Since I began to speak
   (And what I say is true),
It's all gone out of my poor head, —
   And so good-bye to you!

What is Tommy running for,
Running for,
Running for?
What is Tommy running for,
On this fine day?

Jimmy will run after Tommy,
After Tommy,
After Tommy;
That's what Tommy's running for,
On this fine day.

KG

70

Little baby, if I threw
This fair blossom down on you,
Would you catch it as you stand,
Holding up each tiny hand,
Looking out of those grey eyes,
Where such deep, deep wonder lies?

KG

71

The finest, biggest fish, you see,
Will be the trout that's caught by me;
But if the monster will not bite,
Why, then I'll hook a little mite.

My house is red — a little house,
　A happy child am I,
I laugh and play the livelong day
　I hardly ever cry.

I have a tree, a green, green tree,
　To shade me from the sun;
And under it I often sit,
　When all my work is done.

My little basket I will take,
　And trip into the town;
When next I'm there I'll buy some cake,
　And spend my bright half-crown.

K.G

Little Polly Flinders
Sat on the cinders,
Warming her little toes;
Her mother came and caught her,
And whipp'd her little daughter,
For spoiling her nice new clothes.

Hush-a-bye, baby, on the tree top,
When the wind blows the cradle will rock;
When the bough breaks the cradle will fall,
And down comes baby and cradle and all.

Curly Locks, Curly Locks, wilt thou be mine?
Thou shalt not wash dishes nor yet feed the swine,
But sit on a cushion and sew a fine seam,
And feed upon strawberries, sugar, and cream.

Sing a song of sixpence, a pocket full of rye,
Four-and-twenty blackbirds baked in a pie;
When the pie was open'd the birds began to sing,
Was not that a dainty dish to set before a King.

Where are you going to, my pretty maid?
I'm going a-milking, Sir, she said.
May I go with you, my pretty maid?
You're kindly welcome, Sir, she said.
Who is your father, my pretty maid?
My father's a farmer, Sir, she said.
Say will you marry me, my pretty maid?
Yes, if you please, kind Sir, she said.
What is your fortune, my pretty maid?
My face is my fortune, kind Sir, she said.
Then I won't marry you, my pretty maid!
Nobody ask'd you, Sir, she said.

Pussy Cat, Pussy Cat, where have you been?
I've been to London to look at the Queen.
Pussy Cat, Pussy Cat, what did you there?
I frighten'd a little mouse under the chair.